leapfrog

Rumpelstiltskin

First published in 2005 by
Franklin Watts
96 Leonard Street
London
EC2A 4XD

Franklin Watts Australia
Level 17/207 Kent Street
Sydney
NSW 2000

Text © Barrie Wade 2005
Illustration © Neil Chapman 2005

A CIP catalogue record for this book is available
from the British Library.

ISBN 0 7496 6153 4 (hbk)
ISBN 0 7496 6165 8 (pbk)

Series Editor: Jackie Hamley
Series Advisor: Dr Barrie Wade
Series Designer: Peter Scoulding

Printed in China

Rumpelstiltskin

Retold by Barrie Wade

Illustrated by Neil Chapman

W
FRANKLIN WATTS
LONDON·SYDNEY

Long ago, a foolish miller
told the King: "My daughter
can spin straw into gold."

The King locked the miller's daughter into a room full of straw.

"Spin this straw into gold by morning!" he ordered.

The girl wept. She didn't know how! Then a strange little man appeared.

"Give me your necklace,
and I will spin all this into
gold," he said. And he did!

The next night, the greedy
King locked the girl into a
bigger room full of straw.

Again, the girl wept.
And again, the little
man appeared.

"Give me your ring and I will spin all this straw into gold," he said.

And again, he did!

On the third night, the King locked the girl into a huge room full of straw.

"Spin all of this into gold and I shall make you my Queen," he said.

Again the little man appeared. "I have nothing left to give," wept the girl.

"You can give me your first child," said the little man. The girl promised.

17

So the King married the miller's daughter. Soon they had a beautiful child.

Then the little man appeared. "You promised me your child," he said.

"No!" wept the Queen.
"A promise is a promise,"
said the little man.

"But if you can guess my name in three days, then you can keep your child."

The Queen sent
messengers to find all
the names in the world.

She tried many names,
but the little man said
"No!" to each one.

On the second day, the
Queen tried even more
names. But the little man
said "No!" to all of them.

That night, a messenger
saw a strange little man
singing by a fire in
the woods.

"The Queen won't win
the guessing game,
for RUMPELSTILTSKIN
is my name!" he sang.

When the little man
appeared on the third day,
he was sure he had won.

Then the Queen said:

"Hello Rumpelstiltskin!"

The little man was very angry. He stamped his foot so hard that he went right through the floor – and was never seen again.

31

Leapfrog has been specially designed to fit the requirements of the National Literacy Strategy. It offers real books for beginning readers by top authors and illustrators.

There are 37 Leapfrog stories to choose from:

The Bossy Cockerel
ISBN 0 7496 3828 1

Bill's Baggy Trousers
ISBN 0 7496 3829 X

Mr Spotty's Potty
ISBN 0 7496 3831 1

Little Joe's Big Race
ISBN 0 7496 3832 X

The Little Star
ISBN 0 7496 3833 8

The Cheeky Monkey
ISBN 0 7496 3830 3

Selfish Sophie
ISBN 0 7496 4385 4

Recycled!
ISBN 0 7496 4388 9

Felix on the Move
ISBN 0 7496 4387 0

Pippa and Poppa
ISBN 0 7496 4386 2

Jack's Party
ISBN 0 7496 4389 7

The Best Snowman
ISBN 0 7496 4390 0

Eight Enormous Elephants
ISBN 0 7496 4634 9

Mary and the Fairy
ISBN 0 7496 4633 0

The Crying Princess
ISBN 0 7496 4632 2

Jasper and Jess
ISBN 0 7496 4081 2

The Lazy Scarecrow
ISBN 0 7496 4082 0

The Naughty Puppy
ISBN 0 7496 4383 8

Freddie's Fears
ISBN 0 7496 4382 X

Cinderella
ISBN 0 7496 4228 9

The Three Little Pigs
ISBN 0 7496 4227 0

Jack and the Beanstalk
ISBN 0 7496 4229 7

The Three Billy Goats Gruff
ISBN 0 7496 4226 2

Goldilocks and the Three Bears
ISBN 0 7496 4225 4

Little Red Riding Hood
ISBN 0 7496 4224 6

Rapunzel
ISBN 0 7496 6147 X*
ISBN 0 7496 6159 3

Snow White
ISBN 0 7496 6149 6*
ISBN 0 7496 6161 5

The Emperor's New Clothes
ISBN 0 7496 6151 8*
ISBN 0 7496 6163 1

The Pied Piper of Hamelin
ISBN 0 7496 6152 6*
ISBN 0 7496 6164 X

Hansel and Gretel
ISBN 0 7496 6150 X*
ISBN 0 7496 6162 3

The Sleeping Beauty
ISBN 0 7496 6148 8*
ISBN 0 7496 6160 7

Rumpelstiltskin
ISBN 0 7496 6153 4*
ISBN 0 7496 6165 8

The Ugly Duckling
ISBN 0 7496 6154 2*
ISBN 0 7496 6166 6

Puss in Boots
ISBN 0 7496 6155 0*
ISBN 0 7496 6167 4

The Frog Prince
ISBN 0 7496 6156 9*
ISBN 0 7496 6168 2

The Princess and the Pea
ISBN 0 7496 6157 7*
ISBN 0 7496 6169 0

Dick Whittington
ISBN 0 7496 6158 5*
ISBN 0 7496 6170 4

* hardback